W9-DCW-383

Athena

by Nancy Loewen

Consultant:
Kenneth F. Kitchell Jr., Ph.D.
Department of Classics
University of Massachusetts, Amherst

RiverFront Books
an imprint of Franklin Watts
A Division of Grolier Publishing
New York   London   Hong Kong   Sydney
Danbury, Connecticut

RiverFront Books
http://publishing.grolier.com

Printed in the United States of America.
Published simultaneously in Canada.

Library of Congress Cataloging-in-Publication Data
Loewen, Nancy, 1964–
Athena/by Nancy Loewen
p. cm.—(Greek and Roman mythology)
Includes bibliographical references and index.
Summary: Surveys classical mythology, discussing the relationship between Greek and Roman myths, and describes the birth and life of the goddess Athena.
ISBN 0-7368-0048-4
1. Athena (Greek deity)—Juvenile literature. [1. Athena (Greek deity) 2. Mythology, Greek. 3. Mythology, Roman.] I. Title. II. Series.
BL820.M6L64 1999
292.2'114—dc21

98-35117
CIP
AC

Editorial Credits
Christy Steele, editor; Clay Schotzko/Icon Productions, cover designer; Timothy Halldin, illustrator; Sheri Gosewisch, photo researcher

Photo Credits
Archive Photos, 17, 28, 32, 34
Art Resource/Nimatal Lah, cover; Scala, 4, 20, 26, 36; Erich Lessing, 18, 38
Corbis-Bettmann, 14
Visuals Unlimited/Bruce Berg, 22; Jeff Greenberg, 24; W. J. Weber, 31; Mark E. Gibson, 41; Cheryl Hogue, 42
William B. Folsom, 11

Table of Contents

This book is illustrated with photographs of statues, paintings, illustrations, and other artwork about mythology by artists from both ancient and modern times.

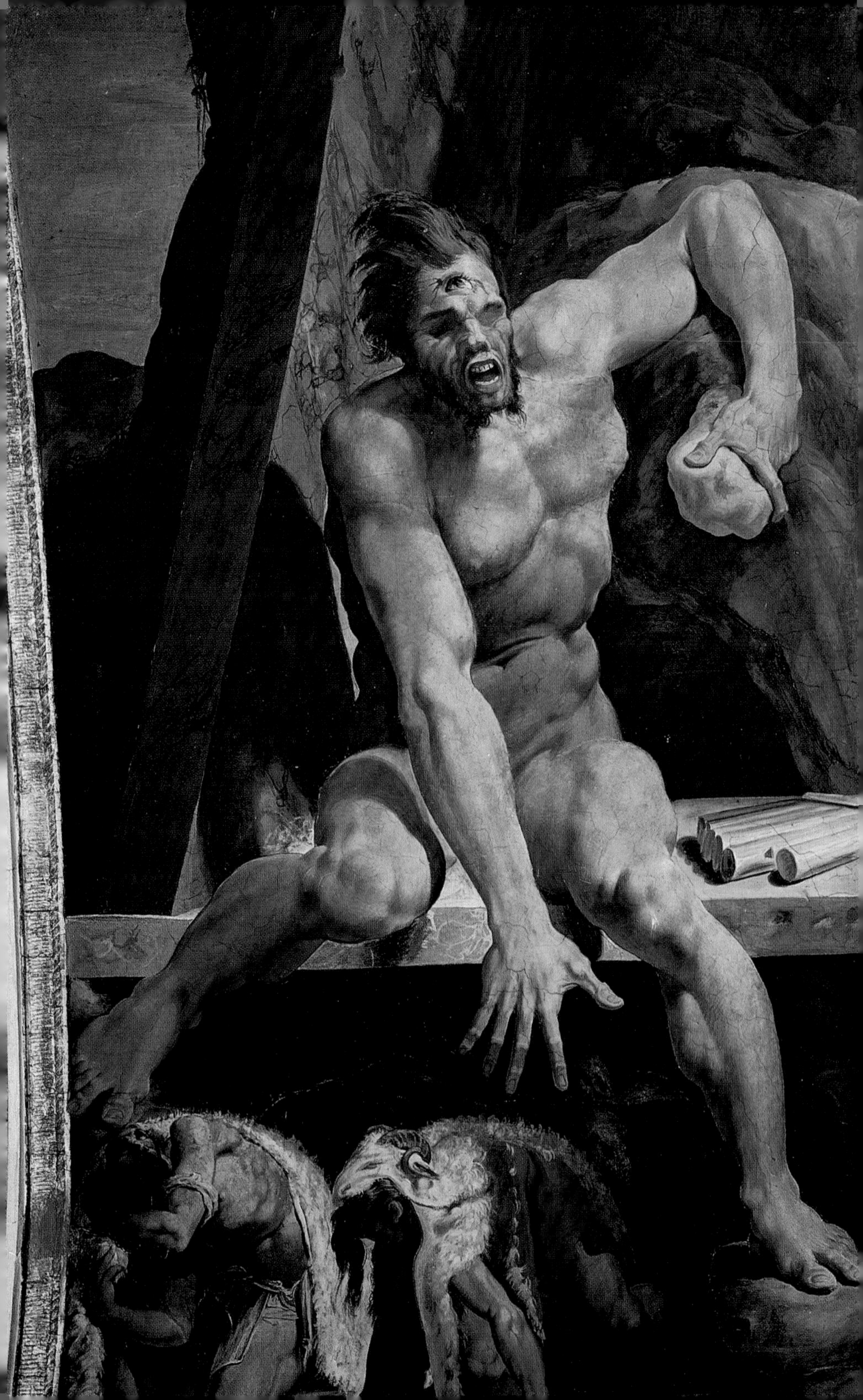

Chapter One

About Mythology

Ancient Greek and Roman people told stories to create order and understanding in their lives. Most people did not know much about science. Their stories used characters to explain things in nature. People understood these characters and why the characters did things. This made the world seem more familiar and less frightening.

Gods, goddesses, heroes, and monsters were the main characters in Greek and Roman stories. Ancient people believed these powerful beings influenced history and the natural world.

These stories are called myths because people today do not believe them. People now use science to explain why things happen in nature. But long ago, the stories served an important purpose. The collection of the

Greek and Roman people believed that gods, goddesses, heroes, and monsters controlled the world.

hundreds of Greek and Roman myths is called classical mythology.

There are two main kinds of myths. Explanation myths tell how and why things happen. For example, one Greek myth tells why spiders make webs.

Characters search for something in quest myths. The search may be for treasure or for a person. Heroes were the main characters in quest myths. They overcame danger and hardship to complete their goals. Quest myths teach people values. Ancient people told these stories to show how good can conquer evil.

History of Mythology

Greece is a country in what is now Europe. Rome was the capital city of the Roman Empire. Rome is in what is now Italy. The Roman Empire was a group of countries under Roman rule. The myths in classical mythology started in both ancient Greece and Rome.

Greeks were among the first people to tell stories about gods, goddesses, heroes, and monsters. They began telling these myths in

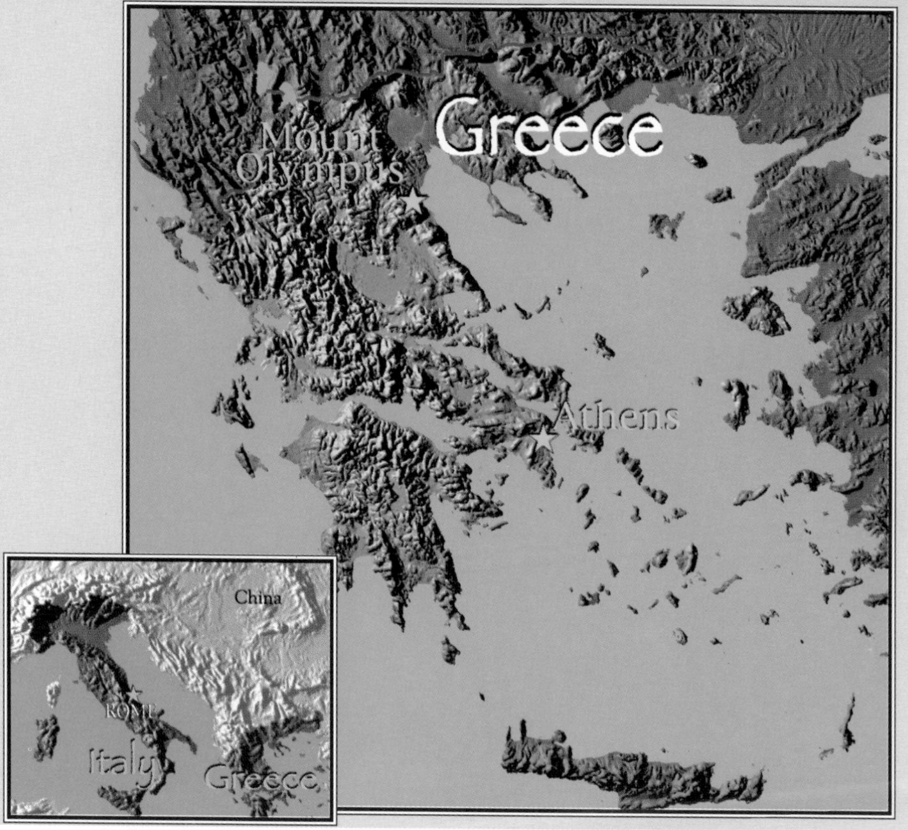
Greece
Mount Olympus
Athens
China
ROME
Italy
Greece

about 2000 B.C. Greek people passed myths down from generation to generation.

The Roman Empire conquered Greece about 100 B.C. The Roman people respected Greek beliefs even though they conquered Greece. Roman people especially liked Greek myths.

Romans began to tell their own myths. Some of the Roman myths were similar to the Greek myths. Many of the Roman gods and goddesses had the same powers as Greek gods and

Gods and Goddesses

of Greek and Roman Mythology

Zeus (Greek)   Jupiter (Roman)
King of the gods and goddesses

Hera (Greek)   Juno (Roman)
Queen of the gods and goddesses

Athena (Greek)   Minerva (Roman)
Goddess of wisdom and war

Apollo (Greek)   No Roman Name
God of beauty, the Sun, prophecy, and healing

Artemis (Greek)   Diana (Roman)
Goddess of the moon and the hunt

Hermes (Greek)   Mercury (Roman)
God of business and commerce; messenger to Zeus

Aphrodite (Greek)   Venus (Roman)
Goddess of love, beauty, and fertility

Dionysus (Greek)   Bacchus (Roman)
God of wine, song, and drama

Poseidon (Greek)   Neptune (Roman)
God of the seas

Hades (Greek)   Pluto (Roman)
God of the Underworld

Demeter (Greek)   Ceres (Roman)
Goddess of agriculture

Ares (Greek)   Mars (Roman)
God of war

Hephaestus (Greek)   Vulcan (Roman)
God of fire

Hestia (Greek)   Vesta (Roman)
Goddess of the hearth

goddesses. The Romans gave different names to their characters. For example, the Greeks named their goddess of wisdom and war Athena. The Romans named their goddess of wisdom and war Minerva. Both Athena and Minerva had the same powers and duties. Both Romans and Greeks told similar stories about Athena and Minerva. This book uses the Greek names of the characters.

Most people living in ancient Greece and the Roman Empire did not know how to write and read. They did not write the myths down on paper. Instead, people learned the myths from storytellers. Storytellers memorized myths and told the stories to the people.

Storytellers sometimes added new ideas to make the myths seem more exciting. Some storytellers told the myths incorrectly. Many versions of the myths exist today because storytellers told the myths in different ways.

History of the Gods
The oldest god, Heaven, and the oldest goddess, Earth, married and had many children. Some of

their children were giants with 150 hands. Heaven and Earth also had cyclopes. These giants had only one eye in the middle of their foreheads. Earth also gave birth to several powerful giants called titans.

Heaven was cruel. He did not like some of his children. He locked the 150-handed giants and cyclopes underground.

Heaven's titan son Cronus did not like his father. Cronus wanted to rule the world. So Cronus conquered his father and became the ruler. Cronus locked Heaven underground with the cyclopes and 150-handed giants.

Cronus married his titan sister, Rhea. Rhea gave birth to six children. Cronus ate all his children after they were born. He did not want them to conquer him. But Rhea gave Cronus a rock to eat when Zeus was born. Cronus thought the rock was Zeus. He ate the rock instead of Zeus. Rhea hid Zeus from Cronus.

Zeus grew up and conquered Cronus. This made Zeus king of the gods. Zeus gave Cronus a potion that freed his brothers and sisters from Cronus' body. Zeus locked Cronus and the other

People believed the gods and goddesses lived on top of Mount Olympus.

titans underground. He freed the cyclopes and the 150-handed giants.

Some of Cronus' and Rhea's children married each other and had children. Their children were gods and goddesses too. These gods and goddesses became known as the Olympians.

Gods and Goddesses

Some gods and goddesses were more powerful than others. The gods and goddesses sometimes fought each other to increase their power and rank. Athena was a very powerful goddess.

People believed the powerful gods and goddesses lived on top of Mount Olympus. Mount Olympus is the highest mountain in Greece. Less important gods and goddesses lived throughout the earth, sky, and sea. Athena lived on Mount Olympus.

The gods and goddesses behaved very much like humans. But unlike humans, gods and goddesses were immortal and did not die. They had magical powers that were almost unlimited.

Religion

Greeks and Romans worshiped the gods and goddesses from their stories. Each person worshiped the powerful beings that mattered most to their lives. Heroes prayed to Athena for help. She often helped them overcome hardships to complete their quests.

Greeks and Romans honored the gods and goddesses in many ways. Some built temples to honor their favorite powerful beings. People brought offerings of money and food to the temples.

Characters in Mythology

Classical mythology contained hundreds of characters. Some characters appeared in many different stories. Others were in only a few stories. Most characters belonged to one of the following groups:

Titans: These gods and goddesses were powerful giants. They were the children of Earth and Heaven.

Olympians: These were the main gods in classical mythology. Olympians looked like humans. But they had magic powers. They ruled from the top of Mount Olympus. Zeus was the head of the Olympians.

Lesser gods: These gods were less powerful than the Olympians. They often were associated with one particular area such as a river or mountain.

Demigods: These characters were half god and half human. They had more power than ordinary humans, but were weaker than the gods. Demigods were not immortal.

Monsters: Monsters could be a combination of different animals or of animals and humans. Gods sent monsters to punish people.

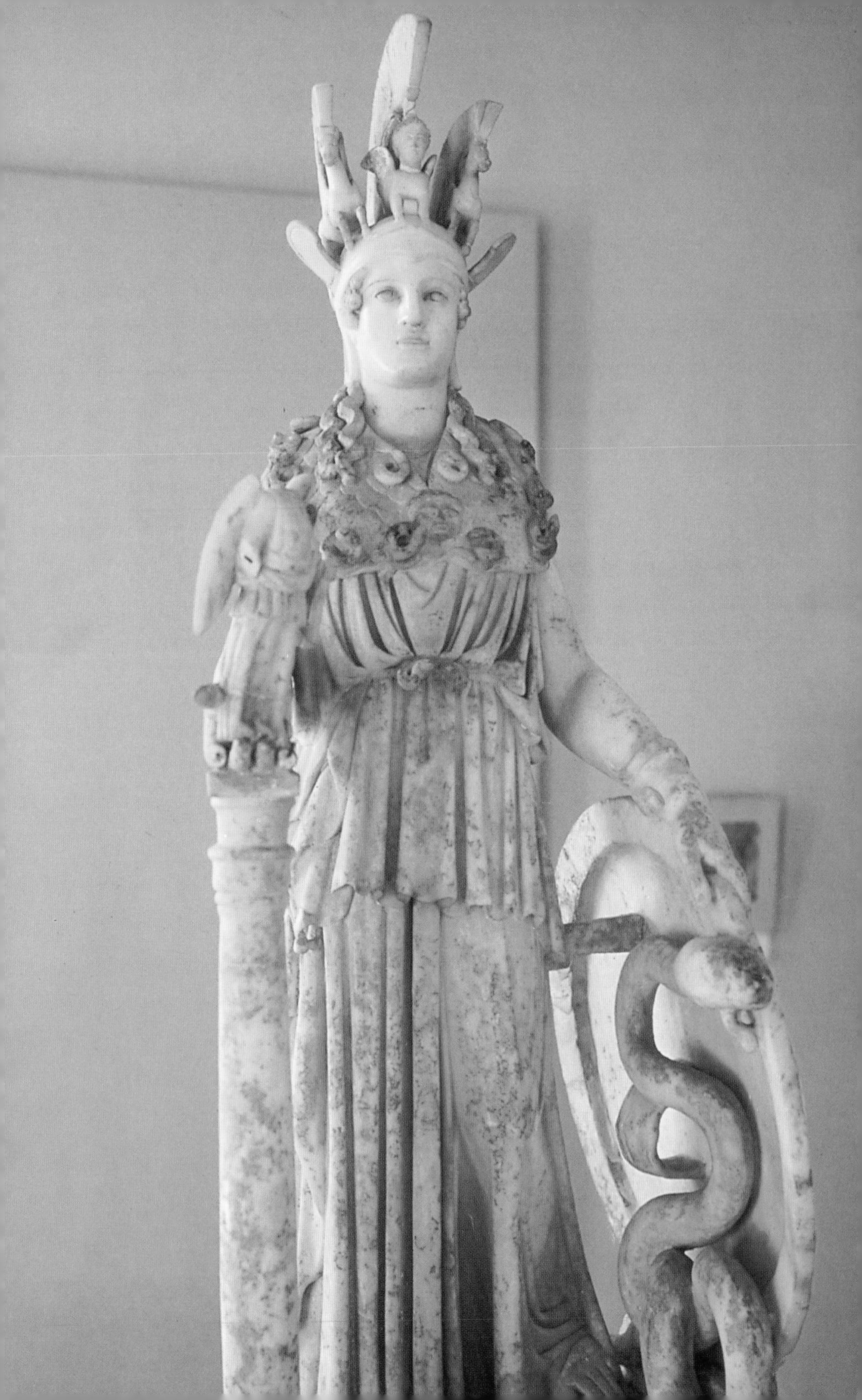

Chapter Two

The Goddess Athena

Athena was a powerful goddess in Greek mythology. She was the goddess of wisdom, war, and the useful arts. The useful arts included farming, spinning, weaving, and playing music. She was also the protector of heroes, cities, and states.

Athena usually was slow to become angry. She hated fighting without a purpose. She believed that it was always better to use wisdom to settle differences. She protected entire armies. Her goal was to bring soldiers home safely. But Athena encouraged fighting for a good cause. She inspired soldiers and heroes.

Birth of Athena

Zeus once was married to Metis. Metis was the first goddess of wisdom. Metis became

Athena was the goddess of wisdom, war, and the useful arts.

pregnant. Zeus was pleased that he was going to be a father. But then Rhea warned Zeus that Metis would have a son that would conquer him.

Zeus did not want Metis to have a son. He did not know whether the baby would be a boy or a girl. So Zeus tricked Metis by playing a game. The god and goddess took turns changing into different shapes. Metis turned herself into a fly. Zeus quickly turned himself back into a god. He swallowed Metis. Zeus thought this would keep Metis from having the baby.

Metis lived inside Zeus for some time. She used her powers to create a robe for her child. She then made a helmet. She used a hammer to pound metal into shape. The hammering gave Zeus a headache. He did not know what was causing the headache.

Zeus went to his son Hephaestus. Hephaestus was skilled with tools and metalwork. Zeus asked Hephaestus to split his head open to find the cause of the headache. Hephaestus used his ax to crack open Zeus' head.

Metis made her daughter, Athena, a helmet.

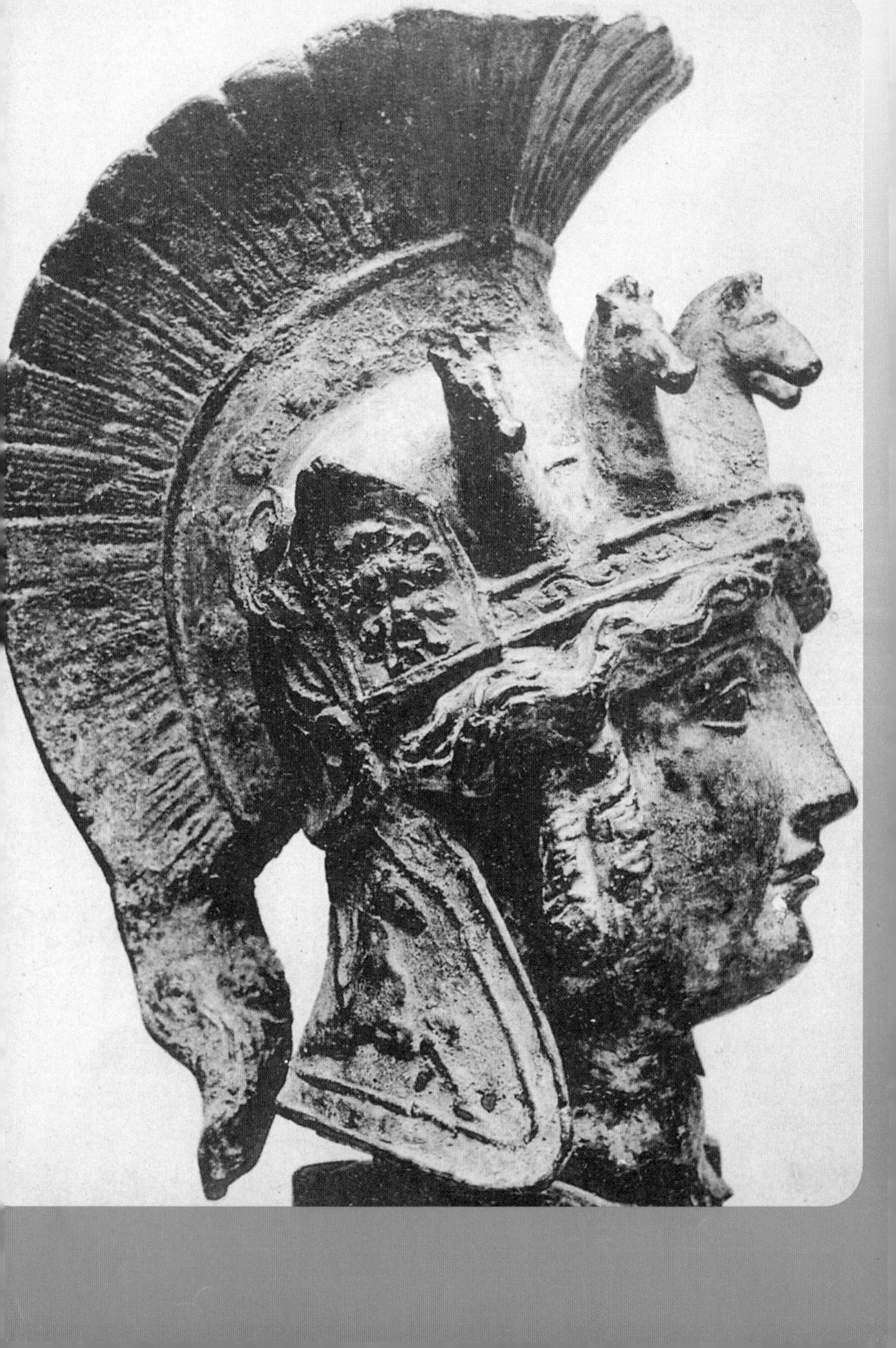

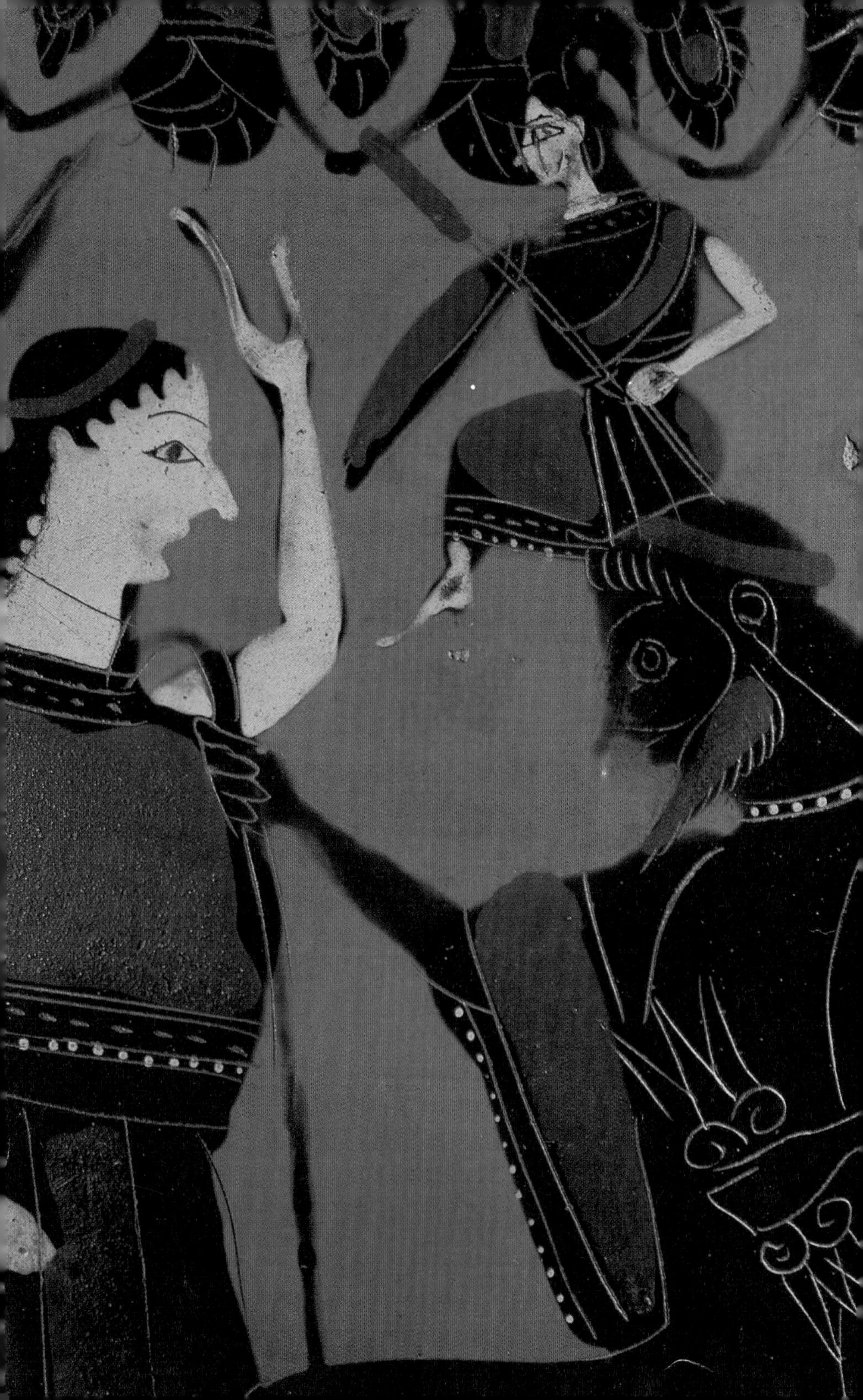

At that moment, Metis' child Athena jumped out of her father's head. She was fully grown. She wore the robe and helmet her mother had made for her.

Zeus' head closed before Metis could escape. Zeus was afraid she might become pregnant again and have a son.

Zeus was pleased that Athena was a female. He welcomed her to Mount Olympus. Zeus had many children. But Athena was one of his favorites. Zeus even let her use his chariot and some of his weapons.

The Aegis Shield

Zeus gave Athena a special shield called the aegis. Athena used the aegis as a weapon against her enemies. It was a symbol of her power.

Medusa's head was on the aegis. Medusa was a female monster with snakes for hair.

Athena helped the hero Perseus kill Medusa. Perseus gave Medusa's head to Athena as an

Athena jumped out of her father's head. She was fully grown.

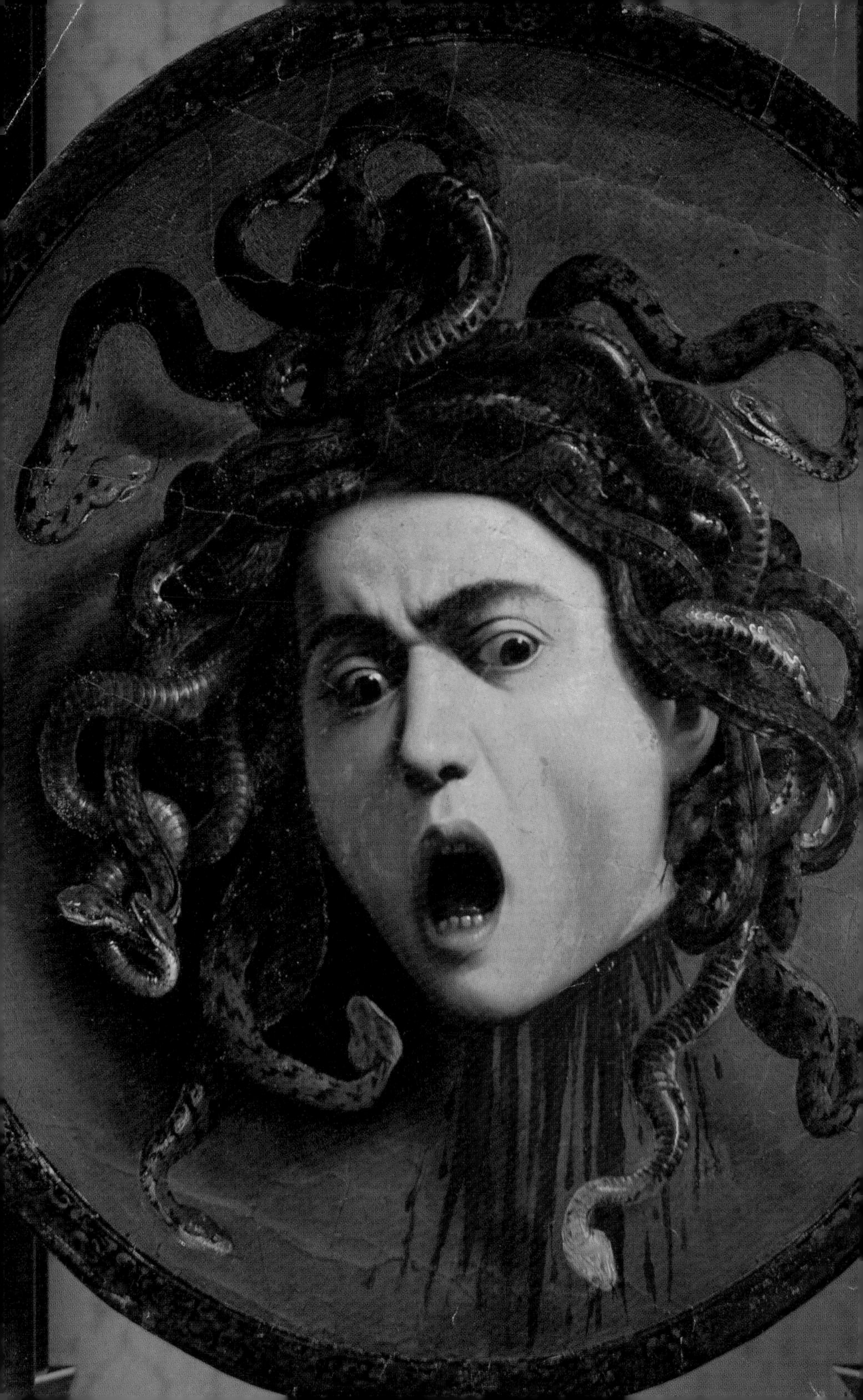

offering of thanks. People turned into stone if they looked at Medusa's head on the aegis.

Athens

People living in the Attica region of Greece honored both Athena and Poseidon. Poseidon was the god of the sea. Athena and Poseidon quarreled about who should be in charge of Attica's capital city.

The other Olympian gods decided to stop the quarrel. They issued a challenge. They told both Poseidon and Athena to give the city a gift. Whoever gave the most useful gift could claim the city.

Poseidon gave the city a supply of water. He struck a rock with his three-pointed trident. Water gushed from the broken rock and flowed down the hill. But the water was salty. People could not drink it.

Athena gave the city its first olive tree. Her gift gave people olives for food. It also gave them wood and olive oil for fuel.

People turned into stone if they looked at Medusa's head on the aegis.

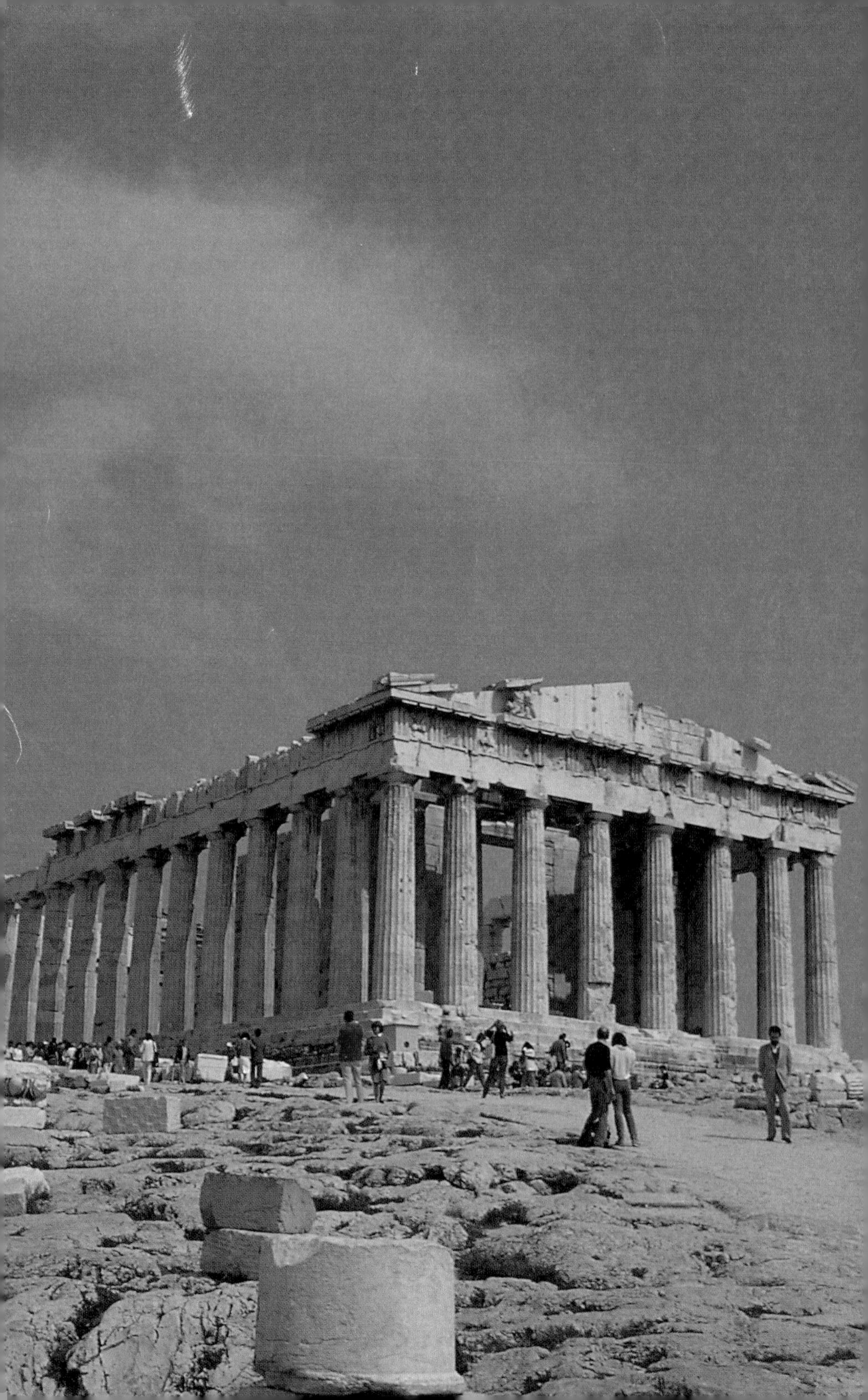

Zeus felt Athena's gift was more useful. Attica's capital city became her city. The people named the city Athens to honor Athena.

The people of Athens built Athena a fancy temple called the Parthenon. They put a giant statue of Athena inside the Parthenon.

The Parthenon was a temple for Athena.

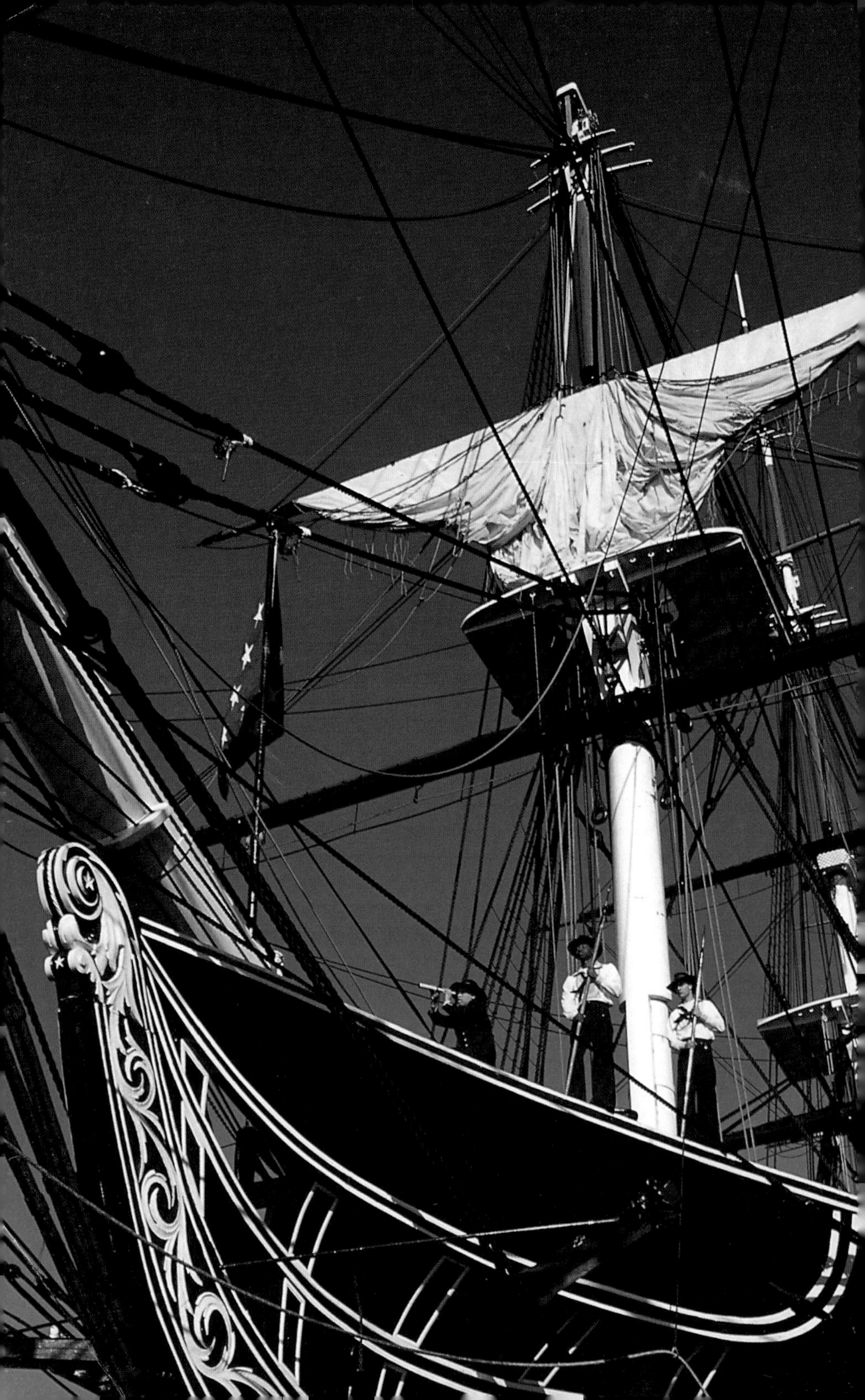

Chapter Three

Gifts to Humankind

Athena was the goddess of useful arts. She created objects to help people and advance human civilization. She gave people many gifts. She invented many tools that people needed.

Inventions

Athena did not favor fighting. But she invented tools to help soldiers. One invention was the chariot. A chariot is a two-wheeled cart drawn by horses. Warriors used chariots during battles. Warriors could travel greater distances at greater speeds in chariots. The chariots also gave soldiers some protection during battles.

Most of Athena's gifts helped people during peaceful times. Athena wanted to increase trade between countries. She invented ships for people. People could travel long distances

Athena invented ships for people.

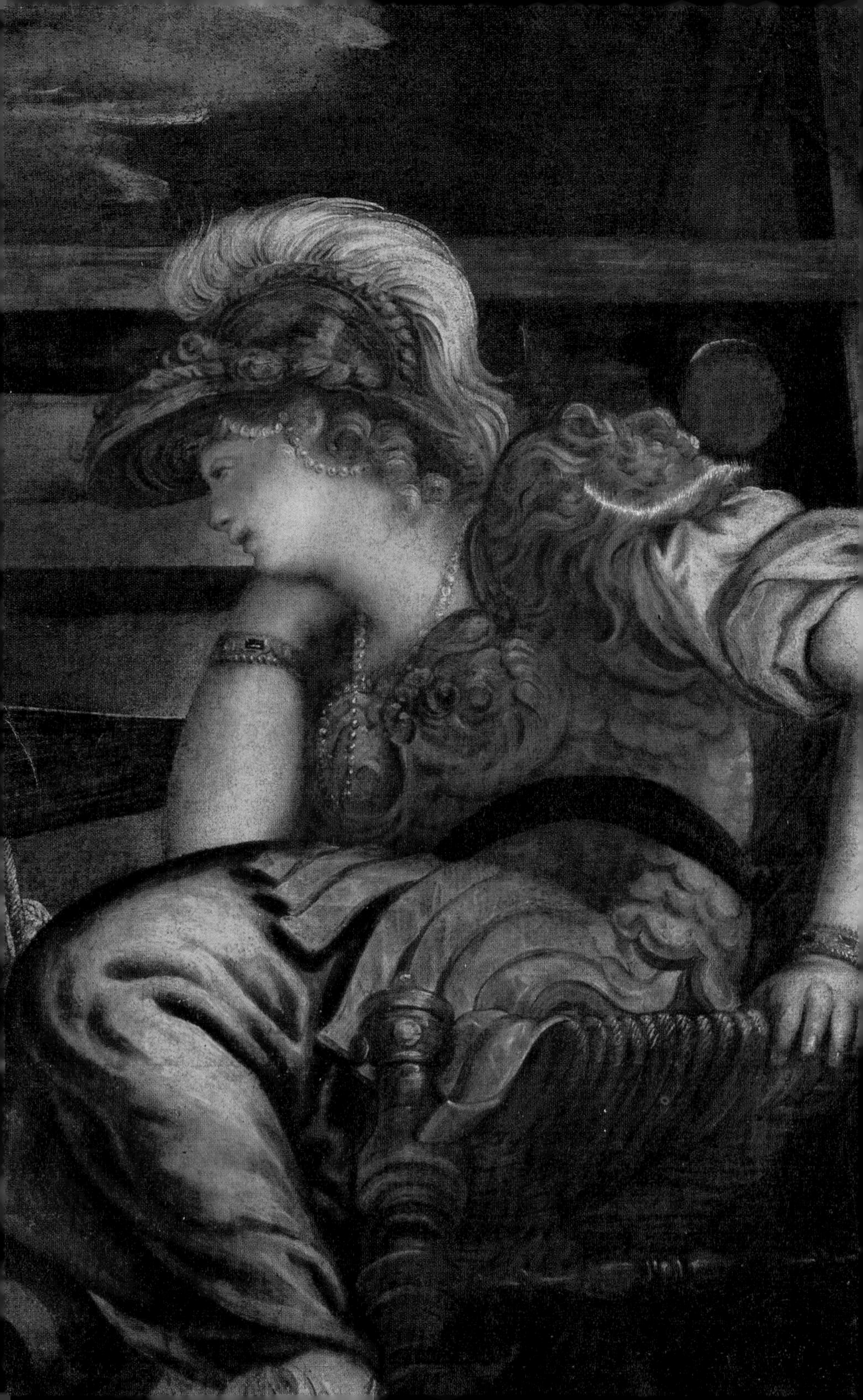

safely in ships. They used ships to transport goods to and from other countries.

Athena invented other useful items. She wanted to give people the pleasure of music. She invented the flute and the trumpet. Athena wanted farmers to grow enough food to feed Greek people. She created the rake and plow. These tools made it easier for farmers to plant and harvest crops.

Athena showed people how to train animals. She taught people how to tame horses. She showed people how to build yokes and use them to link two oxen together.

Athena invented a machine called a loom for weaving cloth. Weavers worshiped Athena.

Athena and Arachne

Athena enjoyed weaving. She believed she was the best weaver in the world. A young weaver named Arachne thought she could weave better than Athena.

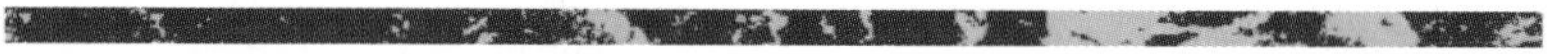

Athena invented the loom.

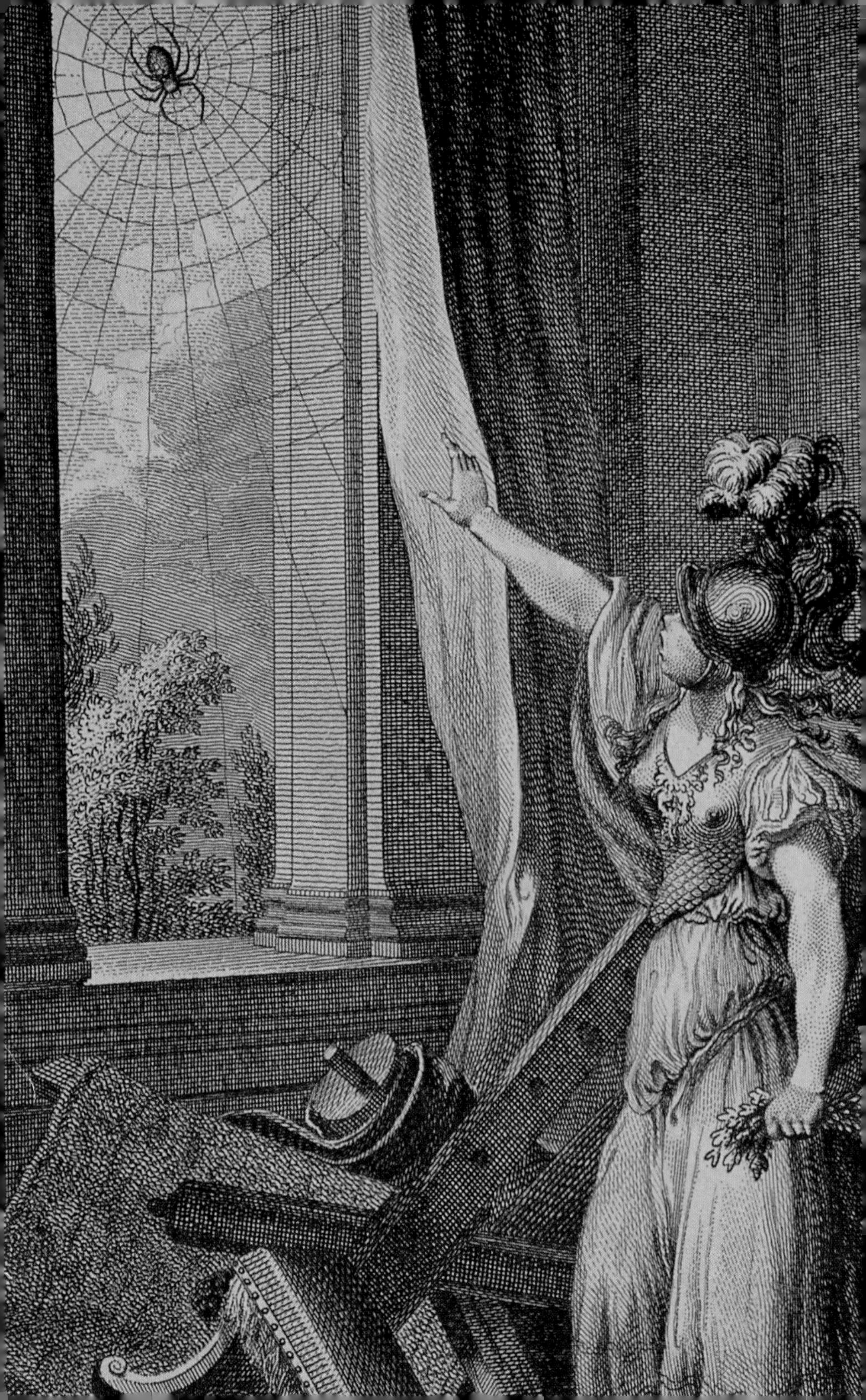

People traveled long distances to see Arachne's cloth tapestries. Her tapestries had pictures and patterns woven into them. They were beautiful. But Arachne's fame made her too proud of her weaving skill.

Athena heard Arachne's boasts. She disguised herself as a poor, old woman. She came to see Arachne's weavings. Athena praised Arachne's work. But Arachne was rude and bragged about her skill. Arachne said that she could weave better than Athena.

Athena became very angry. She changed herself back into her goddess form. She then challenged Arachne to a weaving contest. Athena and Arachne began weaving.

Athena's tapestry showed the greatness of the gods and goddesses. The center of her tapestry showed images of the Olympian gods. The images in the tapestry's corners showed people suffering because they disobeyed the gods.

Athena turned Arachne into a spider.

Arachne's tapestry made the gods look like fools. Athena was furious. She ripped Arachne's tapestry into small pieces. Athena then touched Arachne's forehead and made Arachne realize what she had done. Arachne's pride had made her insult a powerful goddess. Arachne felt sorry for her behavior and tried to hang herself.

Athena showed mercy to Arachne. She did not let Arachne die. Instead, Athena waved her finger and turned Arachne into a spider.

Arachne used her weaving skills as a spider. She wove spider webs. The webs were beautiful but did not last long.

The myth of Athena and Arachne influenced early scientists when they grouped animals into classes. Scientists used the word Arachnida as the name of the group of animals that includes spiders, scorpions, mites, and ticks. Animals from this group often are called arachnids.

Scientists used the word Arachnida as the name of the group of animals that includes spiders.

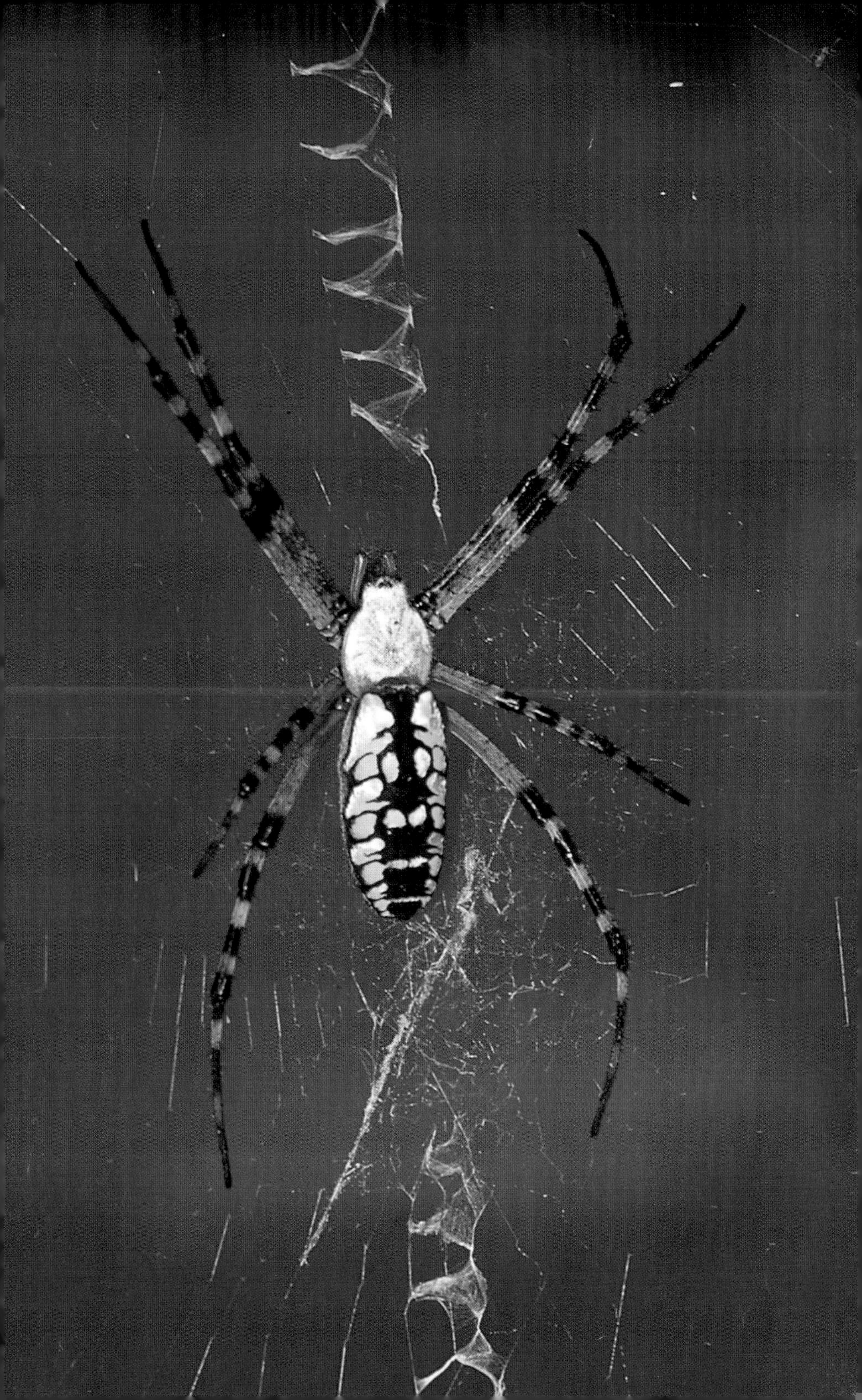

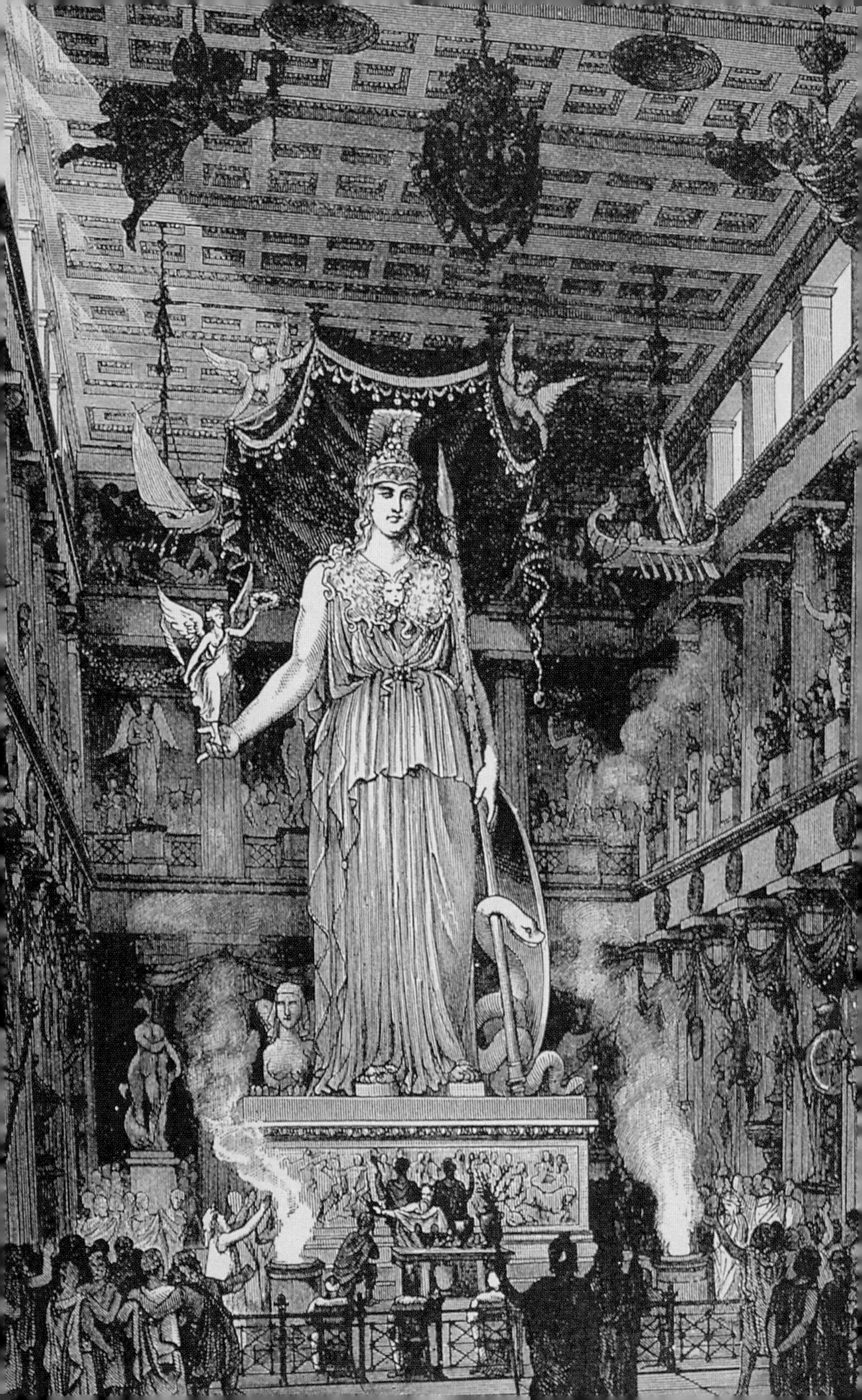

Chapter Four

Athena and Heroes

Some gods and goddesses created problems for heroes who were on quests. Heroes usually met challenges and performed good deeds on their quests.

One of Athena's duties was to help heroes. She sometimes gave heroes powerful gifts that helped them complete their quests.

Bellerophon

The hero Bellerophon was on a quest to kill Chimera. Chimera was a monster with a lion's head, a goat's body, and a dragon's tail. Bellerophon went to Athena's temple. He prayed and gave her many offerings.

Athena decided to help Bellerophon. She gave him a golden bridle. A bridle is a system of straps that fits around a horse's head and

Bellerophon prayed and gave many offerings at Athena's temple.

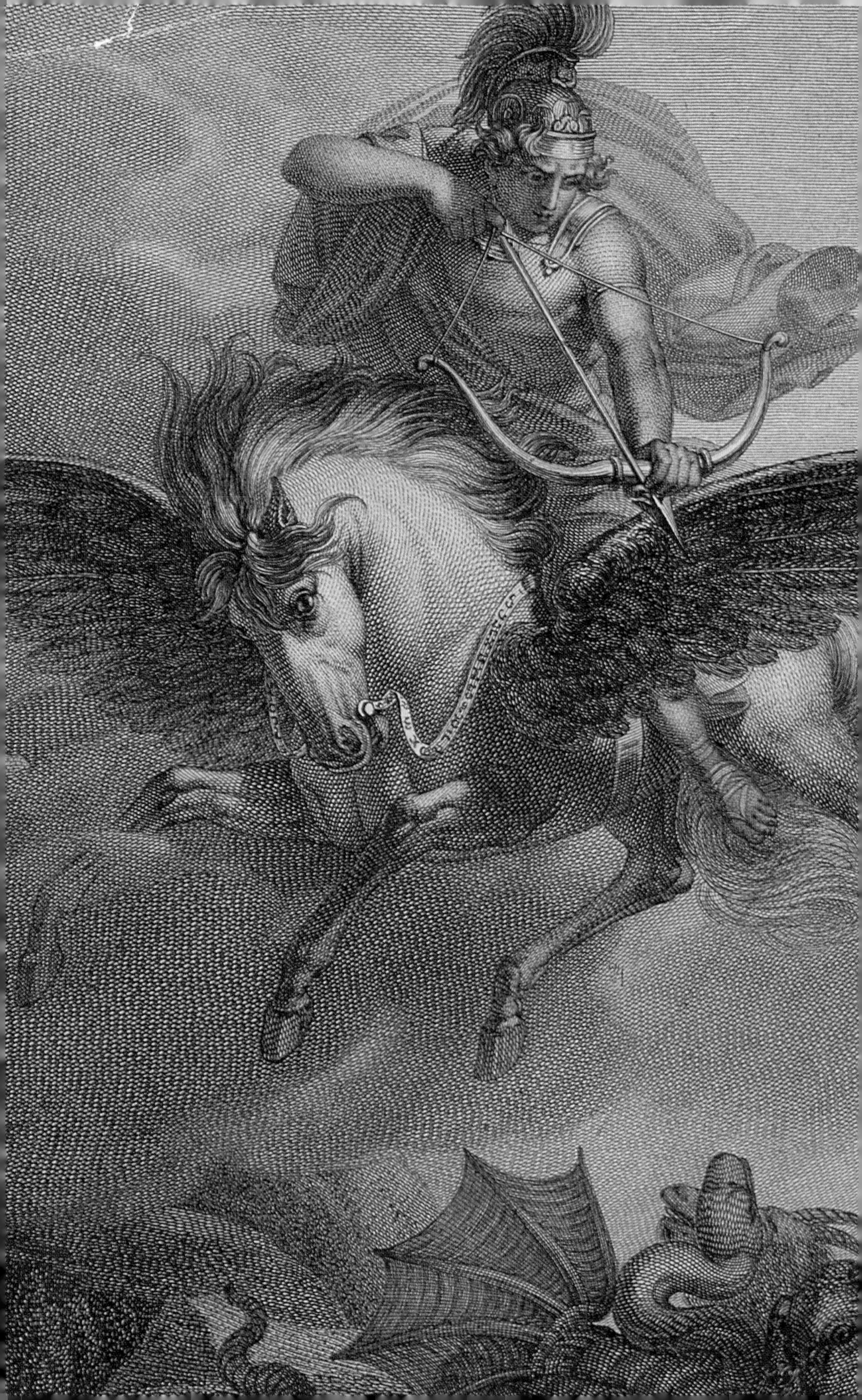

mouth. Bridles help riders control horses. Athena told Bellerophon where to find the winged horse, Pegasus. Bellerophon used the bridle on Pegasus.

Bellerophon flew on Pegasus' back while he fought Chimera. This kept Bellerophon out of Chimera's reach. Bellerophon killed Chimera with Pegasus' help.

Jason

Jason was a Greek hero. He became famous for his quest to find the golden fleece. The golden fleece was the wool of a golden ram sacrificed to Zeus. The fleece hung hidden in a special oak tree. It was guarded by a fierce dragon.

Athena helped Jason on his quest. First, Athena helped a shipbuilder named Argos make a ship for Jason. Jason needed a very large, strong ship. The ship had to carry 50 warriors who wanted to help Jason find the fleece.

Bellerophon flew on Pegasus' back while he fought Chimera.

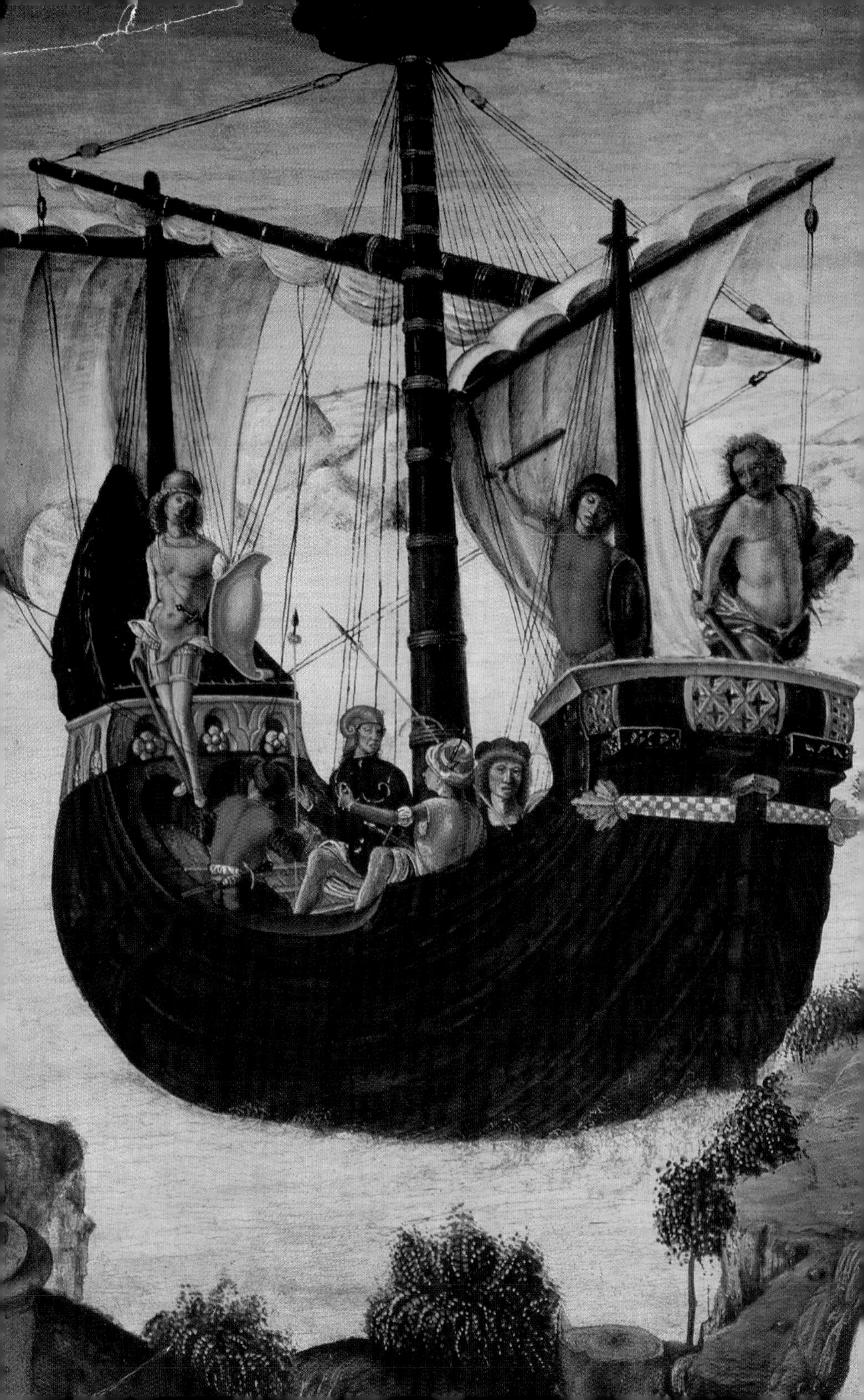

Jason named the ship the *Argo*. *Argo* was the largest ship ever built. Athena made a special figurehead for the ship. The figurehead decorated the front of the boat. The figurehead could speak. It warned Jason of danger.

Jason and his warriors faced many hardships during their search for the golden fleece. Athena protected Jason and saved him many times. Finally, Jason captured the fleece and brought it back home with him.

Jason and his warriors searched for the golden fleece.

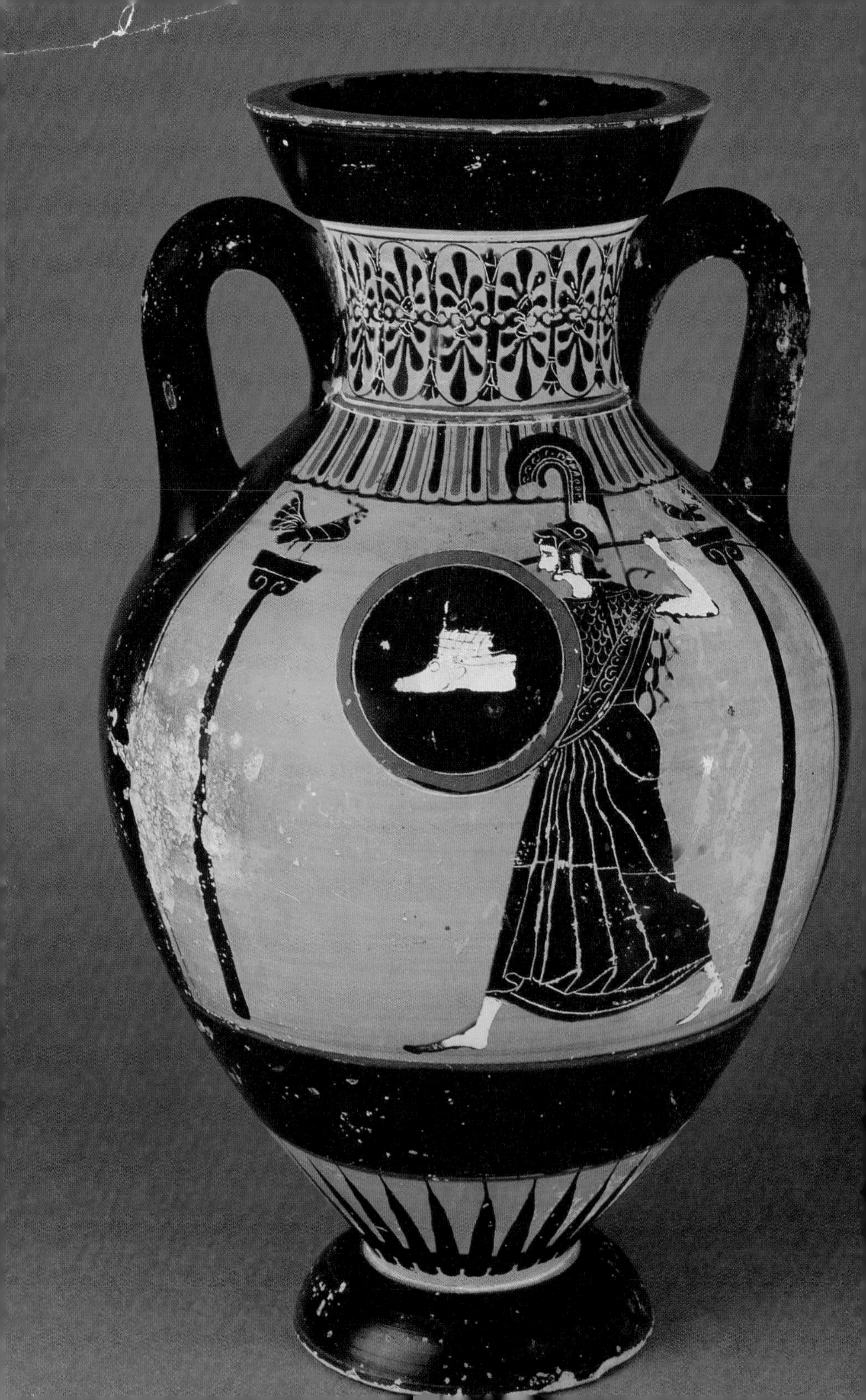

Chapter Five

Mythology in the Modern World

Many people enjoy studying classical mythology today. People can read myths to learn about life in ancient times.

People can enjoy viewing art inspired by classical mythology. Artists painted pictures and made statues of Athena. They sometimes painted Athena myths on vases or walls. Many of these artworks are on display in museums.

Architecture and Stories

The popularity of classical mythology has influenced architecture. Architecture is the planning of buildings. People today often create buildings that look like ancient Greek or Roman temples.

Artists sometimes painted Athena myths on vases.

39

Many builders throughout history have copied the architecture of the Parthenon. Their buildings have many columns like the Parthenon does. In a war long ago, soldiers accidentally destroyed much of the Parthenon. Many people visit the site of the Parthenon's ruins each year.

Myths have influenced books and stories. Famous books and stories often refer to characters or action from myths. Intelligent people in stories often are compared to Athena.

People today still enjoy reading classical mythology. Students often study myths about Athena in school.

Nike

One of Athena's companions is famous today. Many ancient artists and storytellers paired Nike and Athena together. Nike was the winged goddess of victory.

Athena and Nike were so close that sometimes Athena was called Athena Nike.

People today still enjoy reading classical mythology.

Today, a popular brand of athletic shoe is named for Nike.

Athena's Influences
Stories about Athena influenced some modern symbols. The owl was Athena's favorite bird. Paintings and drawings often show Athena with an owl.

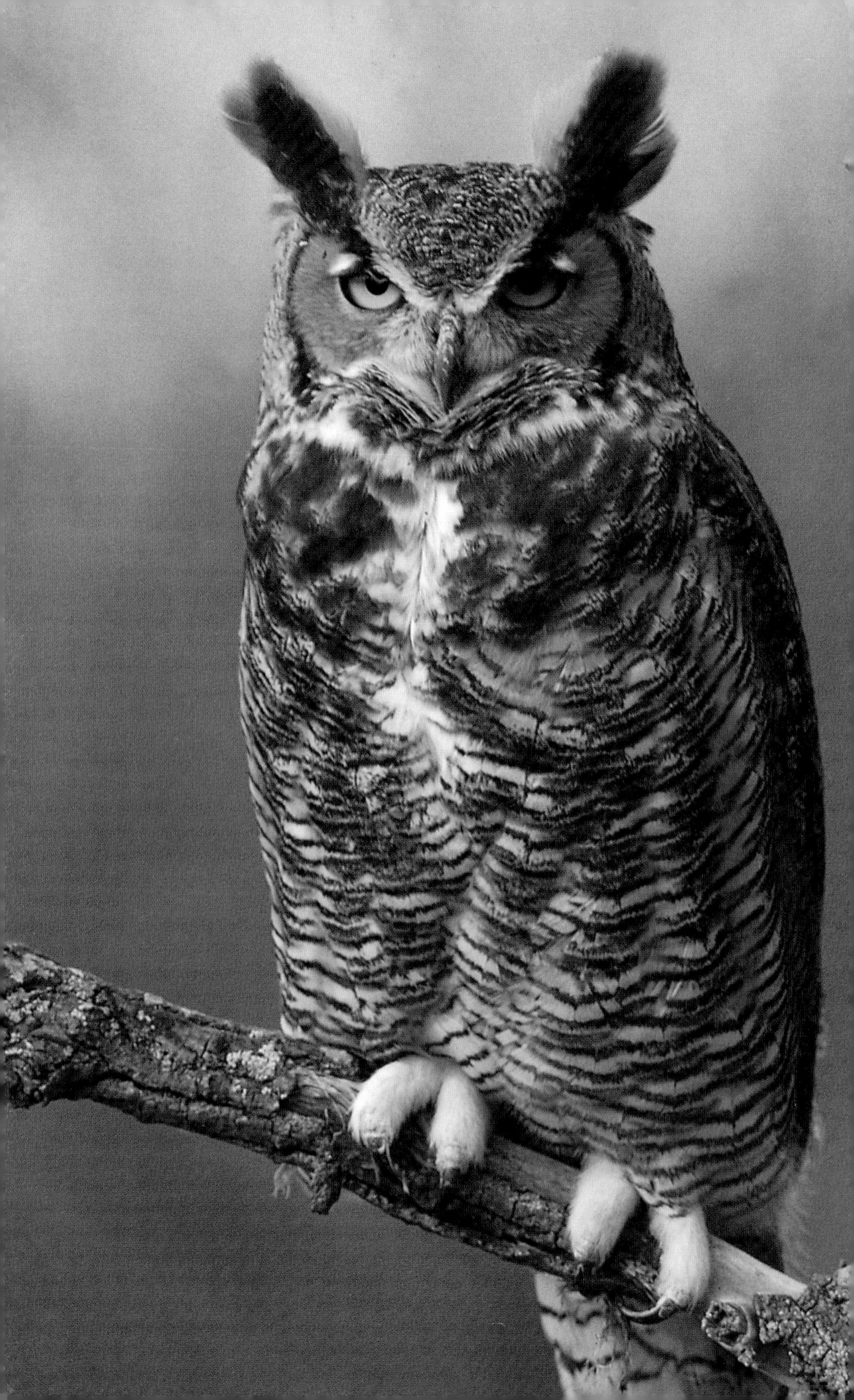

The owl became a symbol of wisdom. Many people today use the expression "wise as an owl" to describe intelligent people.

Test of Time

Wisdom, war, and magic fill the myths about Athena. But the myths were more than good stories. Myths made Greek and Roman people feel connected to each other and to their past. Myths about Athena taught people to work hard and to be wise and humble.

The world has changed since the days when ancient Greeks and Romans told myths. But people still enjoy reading classical mythology. The myths teach people about human behavior and values. The myths also help people today understand the beliefs of people who lived many years ago.

Many people today use the expression "wise as an owl" to describe intelligent people.

Words to Know

architecture (AR-ki-tek-chur)—the planning of buildings

chariot (CHA-ree-uht)—a light, two-wheeled cart pulled by horses

cyclops (SYE-clahpss)—a giant with one eye in the middle of its forehead

immortal (i-MOR-tuhl)—having the ability to live forever

loom (LOOM)—a machine people use to make cloth

myth (MITH)—a story with a purpose; myths often describe quests or explain natural events

symbol (SIM-buhl)—something that stands for or suggests something else; the U.S. flag is a symbol of the United States.

titan (TYE-tuhn)—a powerful giant

trident (TRYE-dent)—a spear with three points

yoke (YOHK)—a wooden frame attached to the necks of work animals; a yoke links two animals together for plowing.

To Learn More

Green, Robert Lancelyn. *Tales of the Greek Heroes.* New York: Puffin, 1995.

Hull, Robert. *Roman Stories.* New York: Thomson Learning, 1994.

McCaughrean, Geraldine. *Greek Myths.* New York: Margaret McElderry Publications, 1993.

Nardo, Don. *Greek and Roman Mythology.* San Diego, Calif.: Lucent Books, 1997.

Useful Addresses

American Classical League
Miami University
Oxford, OH 45056-1694

American Philological Association
John Marincola, Secretary/Treasurer
19 University Place, Room 328
New York, NY 10003-4556

Classical Association of the Middle West and South
Gregory Daugherty, Secretary/Treasurer
Department of Classics
Randolph-Macon College
Ashland, VA 23005

Ontario Classical Association
2072 Madden Boulevard
Oakville, ON L6H 3L6
Canada

Internet Sites

The Book of Gods, Goddesses, Heroes, and Other Characters of Mythology
http://www.cybercomm.net/~grandpa/gdsindex.
  html

Encyclopedia Mythica
http://www.pantheon.org/mythica/areas

Mythology
http://www.windows.umich.edu/mythology/
  mythology.html

Myths and Legends
http://pubpages.unh.edu/~cbsiren/myth.html

The Perseus Project
http://www.perseus.tufts.edu/

World Mythology: Ancient Greek and Roman
http://www.artsMIA.org/mythology/
  ancientgreekandroman.html

Index

DATE DUE
